Also compiled by John Foster

101 Favourite Poems
A Century of Children's Poems
Loopy Limericks
Dead Funny
Teasing Tongue-Twisters
Seriously Scary Poems
Completely Crazy Poems

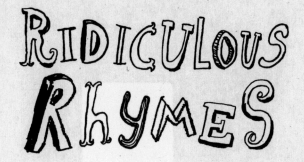

RIDICULOUS RHYMES

picked by **John Foster**

Illustrated by **Nathan Reed**

HarperCollins *Children's Books*

First published by Collins in 2001
Collins is an imprint of HarperCollins*Publishers* Ltd,
77-85 Fulham Palace Road, Hammersmith, W6 8JB

The HarperCollins *Children's Books* website address is:
www.harpercollinschildrensbooks.co.uk

ISBN 978-0-00-711212-8

REALLY
ODD
RELATIVES

My Father

My father *is* a werewolf,

Right now, he's busy moulting.

He leaves his hairs on stairs and chairs.

It's really quite revolting.

And *if* my friends make comments

(For some of them are faddy),

I tell them it's the cat or dog.

I never say *it's* daddy.

Kaye Umansky

Cause for Concern

My brother Jim has hairy ears.

Dad has a hairy nose.

But Uncle Pete

Has hairy feet –

And claws instead of toes...!

Trevor Harvey

Sister Drac

Dracula married my sister

If you don't believe me,

Check.

You can clearly see

The big red mark

Where he fanged her on the neck.

Bill Condon

Cousin Jane

Yesterday my cousin Jane
Said she was an aeroplane,
But I wanted further proof –
So I pushed her off the roof.

Colin West

Andrea Ayres
(A Hairy Relation)

Andrea Ayres was covered in hairs

Of infinite colour and size.

They covered her face and revealed not a trace

Of her mouth or her nose or her eyes.

Her teachers at school were unspeakably cruel.

They called her a fuzzy-faced gibbon.

But Andrea's mates thought her hair was just great

And decked her with hairpins and ribbon.

She was happy for years till her mum got some
    shears

And thoughtlessly gave her a prune,

In an hour and a quarter that hairy young daughter

Was bald as a rubber balloon.

Now Andrea Ayres sheds buckets of tears

As she sits in her night-gown and slippers,

So take my advice which is clear and concise:

Be careful of adults with clippers!

Doug Macleod

The Mad Family

Cousin Frank is off his head
So is cousin Molly
Grandad Bert is out to lunch
While nana's off her trolley
Uncle Bill is bonkers
Auntie Flo's insane
Brother Wilf has shot his bolt
And Marlon has no brain
Sister Pru is really weird
My mother, she's plain potty
As for dad, well he is nuts
But I am merely DOTTY.

Richard Caley

Aunt Brute

Aunt Brute was cute
In a bulldog way
But kissing her was weird
She always took her teeth out first
And hung them in her beard.

Bill Condon

The Orang-utan

The closest relative of man
They say, is the orang-utan;
And when I look at Grandpapa,
I realise how right they are.

Colin West

Kitty

Isn't it a
Dreadful pity
What became of
Dreamy Kitty,
Noticing the
Moon above her,
Not

    the

       missing

          man-hole

            cover?

Colin West

Uncle Clyde's Indoor Beach

Uncle Clyde ripped up his carpet
And covered the floor with sand
And then built some lovely castles
Which he flattened with his hand

He used to have a sofa
But that's no longer there
For Uncle Clyde prefers to sit
In a stripy blue deck chair

He's also fitted a wave machine
In the place where the telly should be
And the hi-fi only plays the sounds
Of brass bands and the sea

And where there used to be a chair
There's now a donkey ride
So Uncle Clyde can always be
Beside the sea side

But *if* you think that Uncle Clyde's
Front room *is* rather strange
You ought to see his bedroom
Done up *like* a mountain range

John Coldwell

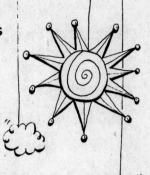

Excuse me, is this your skull?

My Mother said
I should get ahead–
But don't think this one's mine;
I found it in the potting shed
By the 'Deadly Nightshade' sign...

Trevor Harvey

Internetted

Mary loved the Internet

But, as her parents feared,

One day when in computer mode

Poor Mary disappeared.

So, if you check your e-mail

There surely is a stack,

If there's a sign

Please go online

We'd like to have her back.

Max Fatchen

Aunty Joan

When Aunty Joan became a phone,
She sat there not saying a thing.
The doctor said, shaking his head,
'We'll just have to give her a ring.'

We had a try, but got no reply.
The tone was always engaged.
'She's just being silly,' said Uncle Billy,
Slamming down the receiver enraged.

'Alas, I fear,' said the engineer,
who was called in to inspect her.
'I've got no choice, she's lost her voice.
I shall have to disconnect her.'

The phone gave a ring. 'You'll do no such thing,'
Said Aunty's voice on the line.
'I like being a phone. Just leave me alone,
Or else I'll dial nine, nine, nine!'

John Foster

CRAZY CREATURES

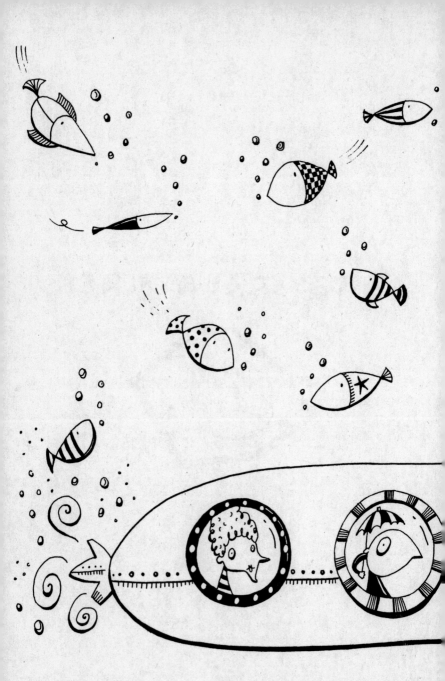

A Baby Sardine

A baby sardine
Saw her first submarine;
She was scared and watched through a peephole.

'Oh, come, come, come,'
Said the sardine's mum,
'It's only a tin full of people.'

Spike Milligan

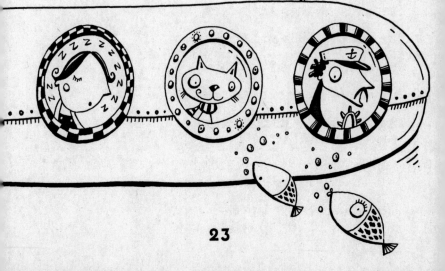

The Rock Pool Rock

There's a riot in the rock pool,
The crabs are linking claws,
Throwing up their legs and dancing
Can-cans with the prawns.
An ancient purple lobster
Is deejaying the affair
But no-one takes much notice
– it's as if he isn't there!

The tentacled anemones
Are swinging to the beat
Of all the little winkles
Stamping all their little feet;
The cockle shells and limpets
Pull apart and then collide,
And a row of flirty seaworms
Does the slinky 'Rock Pool Glide'.

The mussel boys are posing
In tuxedos, shiny blue,
A snazzy razor shell pops up
And yells, 'Hi, lads, what's new?'
Yeh, it's rocking in the rock pool,
It's a swinging seashore jam.
Hey, don't take off your shoes
And put your toes in —
          cool it, man!

Patricia Leighton

Bedbug, Bedbug

Bedbug, bedbug, where have you been?
I've been up to London to visit the queen.

Bedbug, bedbug, what did you do?
I bit the queen's bottom. I bit the king's too.

John Foster

Way Down South Where Bananas Grow

Way down south where bananas grow,
A grasshopper stepped on an elephant's toe.
The elephant said, with tears in his eyes,
'Pick on somebody your own size.'

Anon

Seal of Approval

A seal walked into a health farm
And sat on the counter to speak:
'I want to lose pounds of blubber,
Could you book me in for a week?

My skirts are all tight round the middle,
My blouses all feel teeny-weeny,
With my midriff so wibbly and wobbly
I'm embarrassed to wear my bikini!'

The staff found a personal trainer
And a diet for blubber removal,
And were happy to find at the end of the week
That they'd got the seal of approval!

Coral Rumble

Crocodile

I met a crocodile today
I took it home with me
I introduced him to my folks
Who said, 'Please stay for tea.'

He didn't like the beans on toast
He didn't like the bread
But he liked my Aunt Gertrude
So he swallowed her instead.

Gareth Owen

Moonshine

When a hairy great baboon
Went off flying to the moon
He gave no thought to anyone below.
For as he sashayed through the air
With a bottom that was bare
His rear end gave a pink and garish glow.
Though its easy to be crude
And this story may be rude
There are parts of a baboon he shouldn't show.

Brenda Williams

Bluebottles

I hate
bluebottles on motorbikes
when I'm trying to sleep,
especially the big one
in the army jeep.

Tim Pointon

30

Pink Flamingos

All flamingos keep a feather duster
underneath their sink
so, before they go to bed each night,
they can tickle each other pink.

Andrew Collett

New Year Resolution

It was January the 1st
I turned over a new leaf
It was clean on the top side
But had bugs underneath.

Steve Turner

Neversaurus

When dinosaurs roamed the earth,
So huge, it was easy to spot 'em,
You'd frequently see a triceratops,
But never a tricerabottom.

Celia Warren

Glow-worm

I know a worried glow-worm,
I wonder what the matter is?
He seems so glum and gloomy,
Perhaps he needs new batteries.

Colin West

Why the Dinosaurs Died Out

The reason for the extinction
Of the whole of the dinosaur race
Was that one day the Earth started spinning so fast
They were all flung off into space.

John Foster

Where's the Dugong Gone?

The sea-cow, or dugong

Has the distinction

Of being quite close

To the edge of extinction.

Pushed out of places

Where dugong belong;

The dugong's dugoing, dugoing,

Dugone

Paul Bright

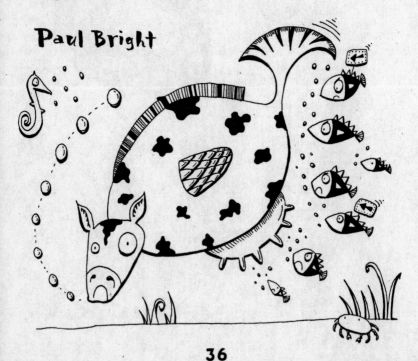

Splat!

No creature can create it
Or hope to imitate it
To do this thing no other beast knows how.

However much they practice
The plain and simple fact is –
No one can make a cowpat like a Cow.

Dick King-Smith

A Centipede

A centipede was happy quite,
Until a frog in fun
Said, 'Pray which leg comes after which?'
This raised her mind to such a pitch
She lay distracted in a ditch
Considering how to run.

Anon

A Milking Machine is a Boon

A milking machine is a boon

To a farmer who keeps it in tune.

But forget how to work it

The thing will short circuit

And the cow will jump over the moon.

Philip Gross

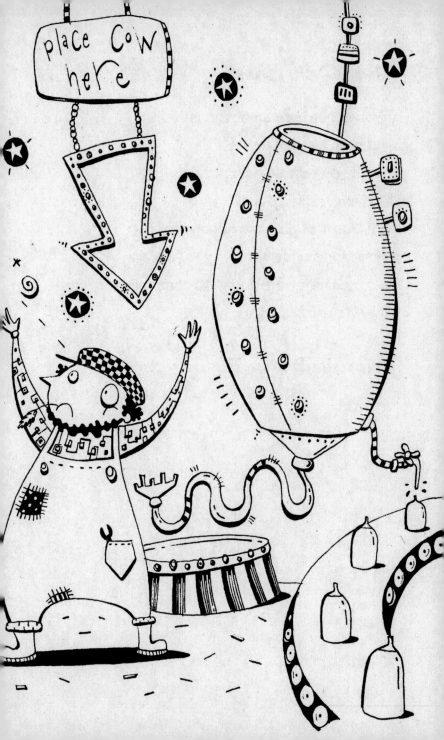

The Octopus

If you should see an octopus

And stop him for a chat,

I warn you that an octopus

Will never raise his hat.

He'll boast of his accomplishments

In kingdoms underseas,

And then he'll bore you with complaints

Of water on the knees.

Peter Wesley-Smith

NURSERY
NONSENSE

Hey Diddle Diddle

Hey diddle diddle
The cat and the fiddle
The astronaut flew to the moon,
He set up a home
In a plexiglass dome
With the dog, and the dish and the spoon.

Anon

Roses are Red

Roses are red
Cabbages are green
My face may be funny
But yours is a scream.

Anon

Baa Baa Cloned Sheep

Baa, baa, cloned sheep
have you any wool?
No sir, just hair,
my dad was a bull.

Dave Calder

Little Jack Horner

Little Jack Horner sat in a sauna;
The heat was up too high.
Said he, 'It's not done me much good but it should
Have at least cooked my Christmas pie.'

Nicky Wicksteed

Mary, Mary Quite Contrary

Mary has a little lamb

But she'd rather have a gerbil

She'd dress it up in Barbie's clothes

And paint its toenails purple.

Lindsay Macrae

Careless

Diddle diddle dumpling, my son John
went to bed with his trousers on,
but what made people laugh and scoff
was his going to school with his trousers off.

Michael Dugan

Mary Mary's Quite Contrary

Mary Mary's gone quite contrary

and given up growing flowers

She's become an organic farmer,

and now she's spending hours

up to her knees in cow-dung

or painting her hen-house pink,

or mucking out her pigpens...

Boy, she don't half stink!

Aislinn and Larry O'Loughlin

Little Miss Muffet

Little Miss Muffet

sat on her tuffet

eating her butties with Bert.

A spider crawled onto her hand:

she picked it up and

shoved it straight down the back of his shirt.

Dave Calder

Mary Had a Little Cow

Mary had a little cow.
She fed it safety pins
And every time she milked the cow
The milk came out in tins.

Anon

A Martian Sends a Nursery Rhyme Home

She sore margarine door,
>   Jellies all laugh and you matter.

Sea-shell live, butter pony away,
>   bee scores, chickens squawk, hen is fatter.

David Horner

Ding Dong Dell

Ding dong dell
Pussy's in the well.
If you don't believe it,
Go and have a smell.

Anon

Smelly Socks, Smelly Socks

Smelly socks, smelly socks,

Where have you been?

I've been up to London

To dine with the queen.

The queen gave a sniff,

'What a hideous smell!

Has someone been sick?

Is someone not well?'

Then she sent us all home

With nothing to eat,

Saying 'Come back next year,

When you've washed your feet.'

John Foster

FAR-FETCHED
FOODS

Nothing Tastes Quite Like a Gerbil

Nothing tastes quite like a gerbil
They're small and tasty to eat –
Morsels of sweet rodent protein
From whiskers to cute little feet!

You can bake them, roast them or fry them,
They grill nicely and you can have them *en croute*,
In garlic butter they're simply delicious
You can even serve them with fruit.

So you can keep your beef and your chicken,
Your lamb and your ham on the bone,
I'll have gerbil as my daily diet
And what's more – I can breed them at home!

Tony Langham

Misnomer

Once I ate a jellyfish –
it didn't taste like jelly;
it didn't even taste of fish –
but oh my aching belly.

Michael Dugan

Telltails

Please spare a thought for poor Louise
Who over-ate her favourite cheese.
Her fate, which wasn't very nice,
Was caused by hordes of hungry mice.
No wonder that we feel bereft,
So very little of her left!

Max Fatchen

Dracula's Diet

When Dracula went on a diet
things just didn't go right,
for, he couldn't seem to stop himself
from nipping out for an extra bite.

Andrew Collett

Pat-a-cake

Pat-a-cake, Pat-a-cake
Baker's man
Bake us a cake
As fast as you can
But wash your hands
Before you invite us
'Cause we don't want
Gastro-enteritis!

Pam Ayres

Runny Honey

A bear in a Chinese restaurant
demanded back his money
for chopsticks, he had soon found out,
were no good when eating honey.

Andrew Collett

Sing a Song of Sixpence

Sing a song of sixpence,
A pocketful of pie;
Four and twenty blackbirds
Baked in a sty.

When the sty was opened
The birds began to sing
Wasn't that a dainty fish
To set before the king?

The king was in his counting house,
Counting out his tummy;
The queen was in the parlour,
Eating bread and bunny.

The maid was in the garden,
Hanging out her nose,
When down came a blackbird
And pecked off her clothes.

Michael Rosen

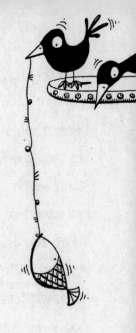

Sling a Jammy Doughnut

Sling a jammy doughnut
Up into the sky,
Splat into a jumbo jet
Learning how to fly;
When the cockpit opens
And the pilot checks his wings,
He says 'Don't throw the squashy ones,
I only like the rings!'

Dave Ward

Custard Pie

I'm Sidney Splatt the custard pie
I love the human race
And best of all I like to spread
Custard on its face.

There isn't time to shout 'Look out!'
Or even 'What was that?'
Before I hit the target
Kersplosh, kersplash, kersplat!

Gareth Owen

SILLY SCHOOLTIMES

The Scatterbrain

'Lost your pencil? Lost your book?
Lost your dinner money?
Soon you'll lose your head, my lad –
That will not be funny!'

Ronnie didn't hear a word
The angry teacher said,
His ears weren't in the classroom,
But where he'd left his head.

Tim Hopkins

Eating in Class

Little girl
Box of paints
Sucked her brush
Joined the saints.

Little boy
Bubble gum
Blew himself
To kingdom come.

Allan Ahlberg

Odd Girls

There are some odd girls in our class
Like Sue whose head is made of glass.

She hangs around with Mary Minns
Whose head is built from baked bean tins.

Now, her best friend is Joanne Green
Whose head is made from plasticine.

And next to her sits Zara Good
Whose head is made from polished wood.

On the desk behind is Cathy Daw
Whose head's a bin bag stuffed with straw.

She is pals with Lucy Moon
And her head is a blue balloon

At the back sits Tracey Dock
Whose head is just a lump of rock.

They think that I am strange
And leave me all alone.
Is it just because my head
Is made of flesh and bone?

John Coldwell

School Dinners

If you stay to school dinners
Better throw them aside.
A lot of kids didn't,
A lot of kids died.
The meat is of iron,
The puds are of steel.
If the gravy don't get you,
The custard will.

Anon

Dinner Ladies

Where do dinner ladies eat
while you enjoy their cooking?
They pop out to the burger bar
when no one else is looking.

Jez Alborough

Science Lesson

We've done 'Water' and 'Metals' and 'Plastic'.

Today, it's the turn of 'Elastic'.

Sir sets up a test...

Wow, that was the best —

he whizzed through the window. Fantastic!

Mike Johnson

Where Teachers Keep Their Pets

Mrs Cox has a fox
Nesting in her curly locks.

Mr Spratt's Tabby cat
Sleeps beneath his bobble hat.

Miss Cahoots has various newts
Swimming in her zip up boots.

Mr Spry has Fred his fly
Eating food stains off his tie.

Mrs Groat shows off her stoat
Round the collar of her coat.

Mr Spare's got grizzly bears
Hiding in his spacious flares.

And...

Mrs Vickers' stick insect Stickers
Lives in a pocket in her knickers.

Paul Cookson

Fear

I'd rather be caught by a python,

I'd rather be covered in fleas,

I'd rather be eaten by spiders

or boy-eating sharks in the seas.

I'd rather be chased by a monster,

melted alive by the sun,

eat bogies, and earwax forever, than:

be kissed in the playground by Mum.

Peter Dixon

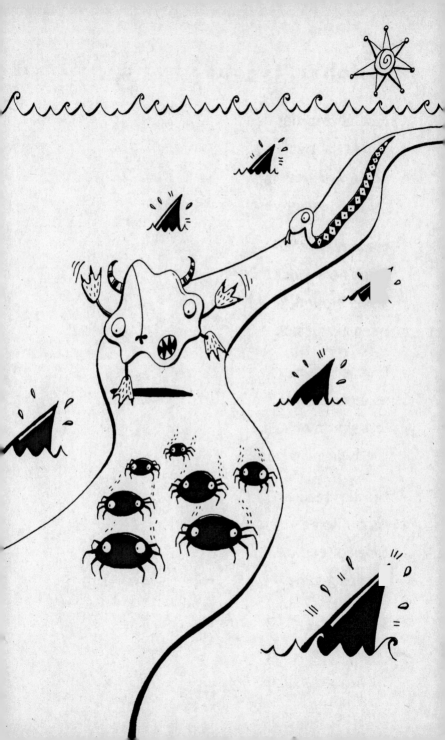

teacher teacher

teacher teacher
you're the best
when you wear
that old string vest

teacher teacher
come here quick
Stella Brown's
been awful sick

teacher teacher
no more school
let's go down
the swimming pool

teacher teacher
I'm off home
time to feed my
garden gnome

Wes Magee

VERY PECULIAR PEOPLE

Electric Fred

Electric Fred has wires in his head
And one hundred watt light bulbs for eyes,
Which means, of course, he can talk in morse
Or flash red, white and blue with surprise.

Just for a lark, he can shoot a spark
For three hundred feet out of his nose.
Wear rubber bands, if you shake his hands,
Or the current will tingle your toes.

Sometimes he chews a fifteen amp fuse,
Or recharges himself via the fire.
Just give him jolts of thousands of volts
And you'll find he's a really live wire.

John Foster

Johnny Went to Church One Day

Johnny went to church one day,

He climbed up in the steeple;

He took his shoes and stockings off

And threw them at the people.

Anon

The Barmy Bishop of Berkhamstead

The barmy bishop of Berkhamstead

Keeps a kitten on his head

Because, he says, his tabby cat

No longer fits beneath his hat

Paul Bright

Elastic Jones

Elastic Jones had rubber bones.

He could bounce up and down like a ball.

When he was six, one of his tricks

Was jumping a ten-foot wall.

As the years went by, Elastic would try

To jump higher and higher and higher.

He amazed people by jumping a steeple

Though he scratched his behind on the spire.

But like many a star, he went too far,

getting carried away with his power.

He boasted one day, 'Get out of my way

I'm going to jump Blackpool Tower.'

He took off from near the end of the pier
But he slipped and crashed into the top.
Amid cries and groans, Elastic Jones
Fell into the sea with a plop!

John Foster

Home Haircut

Nellie, cutting Johnnie's hair,

Was taking insufficient care;

She turned to hear what someone said,

And found that she'd cut off his head!

She smiled, 'I know just what to do.'

And stuck it on again with glue.

John Cunliffe

Little Miss Whistle Nose

Little Miss Mary Rose

Has a most unusual nose

Because whenever Mary goes

To place a hankie on that nose

It plays a tune when she blows.

She's been seen by many doctors

And appeared on TV shows

But why her nose makes a noise

No-one knows.

John Coldwell

Rosemary's Teeth

Rosemary Freeth
Had holes in her teeth
Deeper than ten-metre rules.
So she said with a shout –
'Take all my teeth out
and I'll sell them for swimming pools.'

Michael Dugan

The Midas Touch

King Midas went to the toilet.
He sat there, very glum.
He knew that when he'd finished,
He'd have a golden bum.

Ian Larmont

Little John Was Not Content

Little John was not content

Unless he played with wet cement.

    One day alas in someone's yard,

    He stayed too long and set quite hard.

His mother didn't want him home

So now he's just a garden gnome.

Max Fatchen

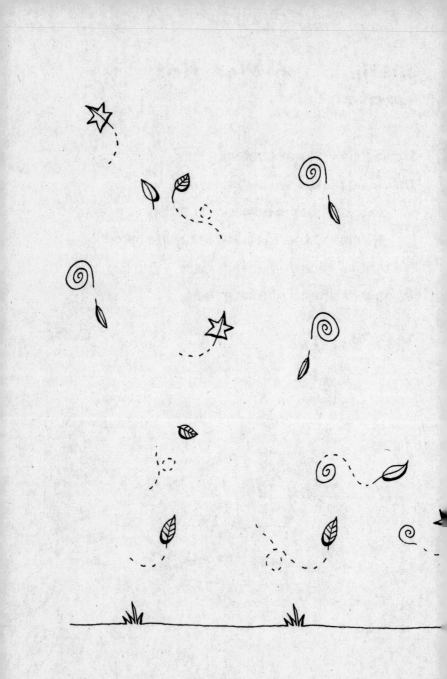

Heather Potts

Heather Potts is awfully thin.
She's lighter than a feather,
Which makes her interesting to watch
In very windy weather.

Cynthia Rider

Topsy-Turvy Street

Our neighbours live at our house
While we live down the street
The postman brings us bread and milk
The milkman brings us meat.

The school bus picks our teachers up
The pupils drive staff cars
The pub is called 'The Dog and Duck'
Its sign reads 'Northern Stars'.

The gas lamps are electric
The village green is grey
The dustbin men leave rubbish
Which we then clear away.

The cats chase dogs where we live
The pavement's in the road
People cut their drives each week
Yet leave their lawns unmowed.

I know it sounds a weird place
But it's somehow kind of neat
I really love it living here
In Topsy-Turvy Street.

Richard Caley

My Name is Tarzan,

My name is Tarzan,

I swing from the trees.

When my pants fall down

There's a terrible breeze.

Bill Condon

FAMOUS FIRST LINES

Mary Mace

An artistic girl is Mary Mace

She paints in water-colours on her face.

Above her eye, the left I think,

Is a ballerina dressed in pink;

At the side of her nose and barely seen

A tiny portrait of the Queen;

On the other side and just as small

Blessing his flock is Pope John Paul;

Framed in gold on either cheek

Are statues of an ancient Greek;

Above the right eye Little Bo Peep

And on her chin the missing sheep.

In italic script her sister Rose

Prints the ten commandments on her toes.

Their master works last several hours

Then dissolve and fade when the girls take showers.

Jack Ousbey

Famous First Lines

1.   Faster than fairies, faster than witches
Runs a rip I have made in my brother's best britches,
And, oh it will need about three hundred stitches.

      All through the meadows I planned a day's rambling,
By hedges and ditches I found myself scrambling,
The britches went west in the bushes whilst
     brambling.

      My brother won't give me the chance to explain,
So I'm catching a train to the Nullabor Plain;
I may never see britches or brother again –
And if that's not enough, it's just started to rain.

2.   I had a little nut tree,
Near the garden wall,
The nuts grew in abundance
But a squirrel ate them all.

3. My mother said I never should,
    Eat mushy peas with Yorkshire pud,
    'I've told you over and over again,
    Put the pud on your head to keep out the rain.'

4. My heart's in the highlands,
    Which is awkward for me;
    'Cos my lungs and my liver
    Are here in Torquay.

5. I wandered lonely as a cloud –
    Seems very strange to me;
    Clouds are fairly friendly things
    As far as I can see;
    High up in their floating world
    They nudge along together,
    Exchanging news about the views,
    Discussing rainy weather.
    Why don't we stand and say out loud –
    I wandered friendly as a cloud.

6. Full fathom five thy father lies,

   His scuba-diving was unwise;

   He would still be here this very minute

   But his air-pipe had a big split in it..

Jack Ousbey

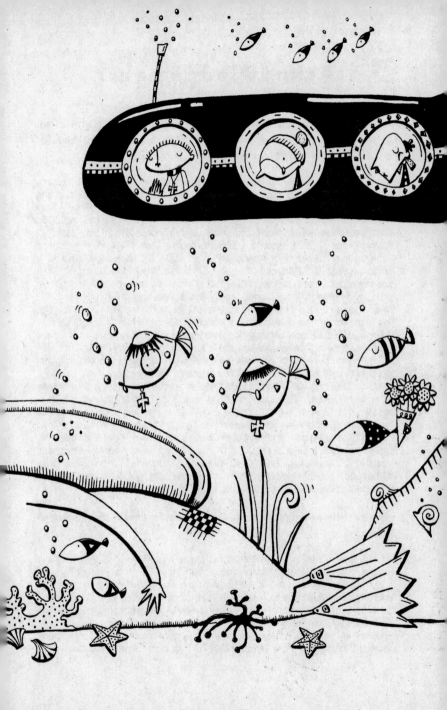

Acknowledgements

We are grateful to the following authors for permission to include the following poems, all of which are published for the first time in this collection:

Paul Bright: 'The Barmy Bishop of Berkhamstead' and 'Where's the Dugong Gone?' copyright © Paul Bright 2001. Dave Calder: 'Baa Baa Cloned Sheep' and 'Little Miss Muffet' copyright © Dave Calder 2001. Richard Caley: 'Topsy-Turvy Street' and 'The Mad Family' copyright © Richard Caley 2001. John Coldwell: 'Odd Girls', 'Little Miss Whistle Nose' and 'Uncle Clyde's Indoor Beach' both copyright © John Coldwell 2001. Andrew Collett: 'Dracula's Diet', 'Pink Flamingos' and 'Runny Honey' all copyright © Andrew Collett 2001. Bill Condon: 'My Name is Tarzan' copyright © Bill Condon 2001. Paul Cookson: 'Where Teachers Keep Their Pets' copyright © Paul Cookson 2001. Peter Dixon 'Fear' copyright © Peter Dixon 2001. John Foster: 'Smelly Socks, Smelly Socks' copyright © John Foster 2001. Trevor Harvey: 'Cause for Concern' copyright © Trevor Harvey 2001. Tim Hopkins: 'The Scatterbrain' copyright © Tim Hopkins 2001. David Horner: 'A Martian Sends a Nursery Rhyme Home' copyright © David Horner 2001. Mike Johnson: 'Science Lesson' copyright © Mike Johnson 2001. Tony Langham: 'Nothing Tastes Quite Like a Gerbil' copyright © Tony Langham 2001. Ian Larmont: 'The Midas Touch' copyright © Ian Larmont 2001. Patricia Leighton: 'The Rock Pool Rock' copyright © Patricia Leighton 2001. Wes Magee: 'teacher teacher' copyright © Wes Magee 2001. Jack Ousbey: 'Famous First Lines' and 'Mary Mace' copyright © Jack Ousbey 2001. Gareth Owen: 'Crocodile' and 'Custard Pie' both copyright © Gareth Owen 2001. Cynthia Rider: 'Heather Potts' copyright © Cynthia Rider 2001. Coral Rumble: 'Seal of Approval' copyright © Coral Rumble 2001. Kaye Umansky: 'My Father' copyright © Kaye Umansky 2001. Dave Ward: 'Sling a Jammy Doughnut' copyright © Dave Ward 2001. Celia Warren: 'Neversaurus' copyright © Celia Warren 2001. Nicky Wicksteed: 'Little Jack Horner' copyright © Nicola Wicksteed 2001. Brenda Williams: 'Moonshine' copyright © Brenda Williams 2001.

We also acknowledge permission to include previously published poems:

Allan Ahlberg: 'Eating In Class' from *Please Mrs Butler* by Allan Ahlberg (Kestrel 1983) copyright © Allan Ahlberg 1983. Used by permission of Penguin Books Ltd. Jez Alborough 'Dinner Ladies' from *Shake Before Opening* by Jez Alborough, published by Hutchinson Children's Books/Red Fox. Copyright © Jez Alborough 1991. Reprinted by permission of the Random House Group Limited. Pam Ayres: 'Pat-a-cake' from *The Works: Selected Poems of Pam Ayres* reprinted on page 55 is reproduced with the permission of BBC Worldwide Limited. Copyright © Pam Ayres 1992. Bill Condon: 'Sister Drac' and 'Aunt